HAZARD PAY

ANNE HAGAN

Anne Hagan

PUBLISHED BY:
Jug Run Press, USA
Copyright © 2021

https://annehaganauthor.com/

All rights reserved: No part of this publication may be replicated, redistributed or given away in any form or by any electronic or mechanical means including information storage and retrieval systems without prior written consent of the author or the publisher except by a reviewer, who may quote brief passages for review.

This is a work of fiction. Names, characters, places and incidents are products of the author's imagination or are actual places used in an entirely fictitious manner and are not to be construed as real. Any resemblance to actual events, organizations, or persons, living or deceased, is entirely coincidental.

Dedicated to:

My friend and fellow author, C. L. Cattano.
Thanks for the title, C. L.!

Rachel checked the address on her phone, took a deep breath, and entered the building.

A security guard stopped her before she could pass through the metal detector. "Where's your badge?"

"I'm with Tech Temps. I'm here for an interview with a company called RHS, Incorporated."

He chuckled. "The entire building is RHS, Miss." He rounded the desk and tapped a few keys on a computer keyboard. "Name?"

"Rachel Bacar."

"ID, please."

She pulled her passport out of her bag and handed it to him.

He glanced at the cover. "Comoros? Never heard of it."

Used to the questions, she answered smoothly, "It's a small country in eastern Africa." With less confidence, she explained, "I'm here on a fiancée visa. We're getting married soon, and I have work papers."

He shrugged. "I don't make the HR calls, Miss. I just screen the people coming in the door." He tapped a few more keys, waited for a printer, then gave her a stick-on visitor pass. "Wear that on the left. Keep it on the whole time you're here today."

"Okay." She looked back at him after she put the badge on. "One more thing? Can you tell me how to get to 1301C?"

Rachel folded her hands in her lap and tried not to fidget while Helena Galatas looked over her resume.

The older woman peered over her half glasses at her. "You've got a CIS degree, I see."

"Yes, ma'am."

"Call me Helena, please."

Rachel suppressed a shudder and managed a nod, but the impeccably dressed woman seated across the desk was still skimming through the file Tech Temps had sent over ahead of her arrival there.

"We'll see how you work out. If we consider you for temp to perm, we have areas where we could use someone with your background though, in all honesty, I see little work experience here." She closed the file folder and laid it aside on her desk.

"I got my degree at CUNY, and I have several certifications beyond that."

Helena waved a hand toward the folder. "I saw that."

"I've also done several short internships and one temporary assignment with Tech Temps. I'm afraid I'm at a loss about what this job entails. The description the agency gave me was very vague. And, I also tried to search your...the company online on my way over here. I found little about you." *Your address, pretty much, which I already had.*

The other woman smiled. "We're a consulting firm. We deal with, shall we say, some very high-end clients who require our utmost discretion."

Rachel nodded. "I see. So, the job is not technical?"

"No. It's quite simple, but very necessary." She changed to a more inquisitive tone. "How did you get here?"

"I took the subway."

"Do you drive?"

"I do...sort of, but I don't own a car."

"Sort of?"

"I've got temporary working papers," she explained. "I'm from Eastern Africa–Comoros."

"I thought I detected a bit of an accent."

"I was here for junior high school while my father was here working with the UN. We returned home, but then I came back to go to college."

"So, you're looking for an H1B Visa?"

"No, ma...Helena." She cleared her throat. "I met my fiancée in college. I'm getting married soon and I have a fiancée visa. I got my temporary papers based on that."

"So, you'll apply for a Green Card, then?"

Rachel nodded. "I hope that's okay." *Because I really need a job.* "The wedding is in three weeks...very simple. I've got about forty days left on my current work permit, so I'll be applying straight away for a green card and an extension of my work permit." She took a breath. "I'm rambling. Sorry. Anyway, I've got a license to drive in Comoros and I got an international driving permit the last time I was home. I can legally drive with it here, but..."

Helena waved a hand. "Say no more. We won't need you to drive often, only occasionally to drop things off to our clients when our usual couriers are overbooked, and we supply the vehicle. Can you start Monday?"

Wow. Okay. "Yes, of course, but, other than the courier stuff, I'm still a little vague about what the job is."

"Don't worry, all you have to do is show up. The rest will be easy. Will I see you Monday?"

Rachel jumped up and rushed to the door of their small Ridgewood apartment when she heard Amelie's key in the lock. She embraced her fiancée with a hug then kissed her.

"You're in a great mood," Amelie said as she pulled away.

"I got a job today!" A grin spread wide across her face.

"That's great, babe! Where?"

"RHS, downtown, a couple of blocks from Times Square."

Amelie raised an eyebrow. "Posh. But I've never heard of them."

"They tell me they're a consulting firm."

"Computer stuff?"

Some of her excitement seeped out of her and she looked away from her wife to be. "Not exactly. Not yet."

Amelie put an arm around Rachel's waist and gently propelled her into their little living room area. "Let's sit. Tell me what you're not telling me."

Rachel sighed as she took a seat in the center of their sofa, leaving room for Amelie to join her. "The service called this morning," she began. "RHS wanted to interview people right away. The job description they gave Tech Temps was pretty skimpy but the pay while I'm a temp there is $25.00 an hour. It's more money than anything else I've applied for, so I told the agency was available to go immediately, and I went. I searched them on my phone on the way over." She paused.

"And?" Amelie prompted.

"I didn't find anything more than the address I already had then, and I found nothing in about an hour of searching back here, either."

"Babe, are you sure it's not a scam? I mean, the pay is low for someone with your computer skills and—"

She waved her fiancée off. "It's not computer work, though." *And it's a start. A foot in the door, as you tell me.*

"What will you be doing, then?"

"Part of it is driving. A small part of it, they tell me."

"We don't have a car."

"They provide the vehicle."

"Is it even legal for you to do that?"

Rachel shrugged. "They seemed to think so...at least, Helena, the woman who interviewed me, did."

"Okay. So, what else did this Helena person say you'd be doing?"

"She didn't," Rachel admitted. "She asked if I could start Monday and they'd show me then. I said yes."

Amelie stood. "I'm starved. We need to get dinner going. As

for this 'job,' I suggest you do as much digging as your beautiful computer brain can handle over the weekend about this company and any name you know, starting with Helena, because honestly, this has scam written all over it."

Rachel stood too. "I sure hope not. We could really use the money. My father has all but cut me off."

"We'll be fine. We're managing. Better than managing, even."

"I want to contribute." *I need to contribute.*

"This is your desk," Sherri Trainor told her as she swept an arm to encompass a large, highly polished, block of dark stained wood with a multi-line telephone and a desk blotter on top of it. A leafy green plant sat in the corner opposite the phone. There was a comfortable-looking chair, but no computer.

"You should have the supplies you'll need in your top drawer. Your job is to answer the phone with 'RHS. How may I direct your call?' and punch the button for the correct person or department. The buttons are labeled. It's very simple."

"That's all?" She tried to keep her surprise out of her voice.

"That's plenty," Sherri said.

Rachel swallowed. "Are there a lot of calls, then?"

Sherri's tone was laced with kindness as she replied, "Not so many that you'll be inundated, but please keep in mind that every call is vitally important to our business."

Which is what, exactly? The approach of another person interrupted her thoughts.

The woman that stopped short of the desk was taller than she or Sherri, even allowing for the tight bun of raven hair streaked with white on top of her head. She wore a dress and sensible, low heels that Rachel was sure cost more than her soon to be gone monthly stipend from her father. Her thick glasses were designer too, Rachel was sure of it. Her designer, no-nonsense look made Sherri look matronly by comparison.

The newcomer extended a security badge to Rachel. "This is for you. There is a scan code on the back that gives you access to the elevators, lobby, garage, and this floor only. You're not authorized on any other floors of the building."

Sherri cleared her throat, drawing the attention of both women. "Rachel, this is Rainy, the third co-owner, here and our CFO."

Rachel thought fast. "Wait, so RHS is Rainy, Helena, and Sherri?"

"Very good," Sherri said. "You're a quick study. My given name is actually Shirley, but I never liked it."

Rainy bobbled the hand holding the badge up and down. "Take this and pin it on your left somewhere above the waist where it's easy to see." She watched as Rachel fumbled with her left hand with the old-style stick pin enclosure that opened to the left and shook her head. "Another lefty."

Sherri defended their newest employee. "We really need to upgrade our badges. I'm tired of putting holes through all my clothes."

Rachel noted to herself that neither woman actually wore a badge. *The privileges of ownership.*

Once Rainy had taken her leave, Sherri told Rachel, "We formed the company several years ago… all Helena's idea. I'm the head of HR–among other things, but mostly HR. Helena interviewed you last week because my grandson had a dental appointment, and his mother couldn't take him. Normally, I would vet all new hires, even temps."

Rachel took a semi-deep breath and smiled. "I hope I don't disappoint."

"Relax," Sherri said as she waved her off. "You'll do just fine. It's the easiest job you'll ever have."

"I answered thirty phone calls today."

Amelie looked at her partner across their little dining table. "And?"

"That's it. That's the job."

"What do you have to do with all the callers?"

"Just transfer them to whomever they ask for. Usually it's Helena, one of the owners. Sometimes it's Rainy, the CFO. She's an owner too. Only once for Sherri. She's head of HR and the owner I like the best. She's the nicest one, anyway. I mean, not that there's anything wrong with the other two women, Helena just seems very busy. She's very professional and Rainy is...she's different. I haven't worked her out yet."

"What do the callers say when they call?"

"Not much," Rachel said with a shrug. "They just ask for the person they need. It's pretty easy since it's just the three women."

"But it all seems legit?" Amelie asked. "I mean, if it's that big of a company, you'd think they would have some sort of switchboard or direct lines. Cell phones, even. This isn't 1970."

And we weren't born in 1970. "So far, it seems legitimate. Honestly, I'd have a hard time telling if it wasn't. I'm pretty much confined to one floor."

Amelie cocked an eyebrow.

"I'm a temp. They didn't give me the run of the building. There's a very nice break room on my floor though with free coffee that seems to brew by magic all day, a restroom that's nicer than any public restroom I've ever been in and it's just... just nice. Everything is very nice. You can tell it's a company run by women."

"So, you like it?"

"It's a little boring right now, but yes. I could see myself working there long term if they put me in IT."

"Well, you say that now, but you're in the C-Suite working directly with the owners. Wait until you see how their minions live before you make any long-term decisions."

∼

Rachel leaned side to side, trying to stretch out her back muscles. *It's a comfortable chair, but I can only sit so much!*

It was a slower day. By her mental count, she'd only answered the phone sixteen times. She'd studied the abstract paintings on the walls at length and counted the floor tiles in the break room more than once.

She glanced at the fitness tracker she wore on her right wrist. Amelie had stopped her from wearing it on her dominate hand in college, calling it cheating on her step count. *Only an hour to go.* Not likely to get fourteen more calls today to equal yesterday.

The glass door into the lobby like area she worked in swung open and a neatly dressed young man walked in. He nodded her way, but he didn't say a word as he moved past her and down the hallway that led to the offices of Helena and Rainy. She was torn. He was the first visitor to her area in two days besides Sherri, whom she'd learned maintained the HR department on the ground floor and had her office there. *No one told me to stop visitors or to announce them.*

Ten minutes later, the young man hustled out without so much as a look over his shoulder. Helena joined her at the desk moments later.

Certain she'd been remiss, Rachel asked her, "Should I have let him just go straight through? No one told me anything about handling visitors."

"No need to worry. He was up here at my request to report back from a client. You won't get too many visitors up here."

Rachel sighed.

"Problem?" Helena asked.

"Oh, uh, no. Not at all."

"You're bored."

"It's fine."

"You can be honest. I much prefer it."

Rachel plunged in. "You're paying a temp service a lot of money to have someone sit here and answer the phone all day… a phone that doesn't ring all that much. It's not that I'm ungrateful, but—"

Helena held up a hand. "I get it. I do. You don't know how vitally important you are, but that's to be expected given the little information you have." She paused and gave Rachel a long look. Finally, she asked, "Did Sherri check your driver's license?"

"Yes. Are you going to have me drive, then?"

"It's a possibility. Make sure you have it with you tomorrow."

Rainy handed her a large cardboard envelope and a slip of paper. "Take that to the address on the paper." She held out a car key and waited for Rachel to take it. "The car you'll be using is a Chevy Impala parked in the garage immediately behind this building, slot six on the first level. Program the address into the GPS on the dash. Use their parking garage. Go straight there and come straight back."

"Do I get a signature or anything?"

"No. Just hand it to the receptionist in the office listed. They're expecting it."

Rachel plugged the address into her phone when she got out of the elevator in the lobby. She did a double take as she looked at the map on the screen. *It's only three blocks away. I could walk there in less time than it would take me to maneuver an Impala, of all things, out of the garage, through traffic, drop this off, and then come back.*

As she passed the security desk, she noted the bank of security monitors. *Everything is on camera. Better not screw this up.* She hooked right around the desk to the garage entry and exit area rather than continuing out of the main building entrance to the sidewalk.

Rachel returned to her desk twenty minutes later after delivering the envelope into the hands of a well-dressed woman in a posh office suite. She shook her head to herself. The woman had said two words to her, "Thank you."

They must deal with couriers a lot.

"I delivered it to a ritzy, as you say, office in a tower so close I really could have walked there and taken less time than it took to navigate the garages and through traffic, but I did it their way. They wanted to make sure it got there safely and securely."

Amelie held the crust of a slice of pizza aloft as she asked, "What was so precious in the package?"

"It wasn't even a package. It was an oversized envelope. Bigger than legal size, but not by much. Very flat too."

"Paperwork?"

"Maybe a sheet or two."

Amelie took a bite of the crust. "A check, maybe?"

Rachel shrugged. "Who knows?"

"Well, a check would explain why they wanted it kept secure."

"If it were some sort of check or something like that, you'd think they'd want a signature. I didn't have to have anyone sign for it."

"I don't know then," Amelie said. She pointed at the last slice of pizza. "Are you going to eat that?"

∽

Rachel didn't have to wait long after lunch on Thursday to be given another driving assignment. Rainy approached her with another envelope and a small white cardboard box, about the size of a deck of cards. She handed her a paper.

"Those go to two different places. The addresses are on the form. Deliver the box first to the first address. There's a Toyota Yaris in the garage for you to take today. The parking is tighter parking at your second stop. You can get the keys from the garage attendant."

Rachel tried not to swallow hard in front of the other woman. *Parallel parking. Definitely not a skill.*

"Where do you live?"

"Um, Ridgewood."

"That works out then. Apartment?"

Rachel nodded. "Yes."

"Is there parking?"

"There's no garage. It's all on the street."

"If you think you can find a spot, take the car home after the second delivery. You won't be needed here for the rest of the day, but we will pay you for the full day. Bring the car back tomorrow and park it in any empty courier slot on the ground floor of the garage."

"Yes, ma'am." *Great. Lots of parallel parking.*

She delivered the small package to what was obviously a medical office in Astoria. The woman who met her at the window in the waiting room was in traditional scrubs. She made a mental note to look up their specialty when she got home.

The envelope wasn't as easy to deliver. She rolled slowly down a street of low-rise apartment buildings a half dozen blocks from Forest Park. Many of the buildings were under renovation, the vehicles of contractor companies taking up most of the curbside parking. *Why couldn't this have been closer to the park? Plenty of parking there.*

She spotted the address she was looking for and a noticed a free parking space several units up. She hoped she could get the Yaris in it without looking like she didn't have a clue what she was doing.

A couple of minutes later, the car parked reasonably decently within the space available, Rachel took up the envelope and walked back to the apartment building.

The front door was locked. There were four units. She rang the bell for one listed on her sheet and waited.

Without addressing her, someone buzzed her in. *Oh. Not sure I like this.* She clenched the key ring in her hand with the only key, the one for the Yaris, stuck out between her fingers then ascended the stairs to one of the two second-floor walk-ups.

An older, heavyset man in dark pants and a white tank top waited inside the open door of the unit. "You from RHS?" he asked.

"Yes." She took a quick peek over his shoulder into his living room. It was neat and orderly.

He pointed at the envelope. "I'll take that. Been waiting for it."

She looked at her sheet. "This says I'm to ask for Lisanne."

"I'm her husband. She's in the can."

He knew to ask for RHS. I hope it's okay. It's not like they give me detailed instructions. She handed the envelope over and turned to go.

"Here," he said, calling her back. He held out a twenty.

She gave him a quizzical look.

"Your tip?"

"Oh. We can't... I don't think—"

"I always tip delivery people. I was one myself for a lot of years."

She took the money. *It's a heck of a tip for such a thin envelope.*

"The medical office was an orthopedic surgeon group."

"Any particular specialty?" Amelie asked as she leaned her head back into the sofa.

"Not that I could tell from their website." Rachel shifted in the seat beside her. "It looks from that like they do mostly consulting, second opinions, and such. They're close to a hospital though, so who knows."

"Weird that they didn't want you to take the car back there."

"Right? And I was so conscious of every move I made while I was driving it, too."

Amelie's eyes popped open. "This is a pretty safe neighborhood. I just hope no one messes with it."

Rachel sighed with relief as she parked the Yaris Friday morning. Even though she'd given herself plenty of extra time, traffic had been a nightmare of delays and near misses. She was happy to hand the garage attendant the keys and be on her way.

She arrived in the office about a minute later than she intended to be there, but a few minutes before anyone else noted her presence. That didn't last long.

Rainy made an appearance a few minutes later and immediately quizzed Rachel. "Did you have any trouble with the deliveries?"

"No. Not really."

"You don't sound so sure."

"They were easy to find. Parking was a bit of an issue, and then the traffic this morning—"

"New York," Rainy said with a shrug. "How did the Yaris handle for you?"

"It was fine. It was a lot easier to maneuver than the other car."

"Good, then it's yours."

"Pardon?"

"To get back and forth to work, for deliveries and such, and for limited personal use. I'll have Sherri work up the user agreement paperwork and go over it with you."

"Um, I think I might need to call Tech Temps about that. I am a temp, after all. I'm not sure I'm allowed to sign off on something like that." *I know I'm not. I signed paperwork with them, saying I wouldn't.* "Can't I just leave it parked here? It's so much easier to take the train in."

"We're going to buy out your Tech Temps agreement early and hire you. You've done a great job for us."

"But I've only been here four days."

Rainy waved her off. "That's long enough to get a feel for someone."

"I only have temporary working papers. I thought you knew."

"I do. Don't worry. We'll help you get an H1B visa and later a green card and handle all the paperwork associated with all of that. We've been around the block a time or two."

This is moving way too fast. "My background is in technology. Programming and application development, to be exact—"

Rainy waved a hand again. "And that's how we'll apply for your H1B, but please understand that we can't move you onto our technology team just yet. We will, of course pay you based on our scale for the tech team. Sherri can explain all of that."

Rachel was about to respond when Rainy interrupted. "Now,

if you'll excuse me, I have a conference call in a few minutes. I'll get with Sherri after that, so expect to spend some time in HR today. Don't worry about the phones when she calls for you."

∼

Rachel took a bite of her Greek salad, but then had to cover her mouth with her hand as she laughed at Amelie who was failing miserably at keeping all of her toppings from sliding off her oversized burger every time she lifted it. "You're lucky you decided on take out instead of us going down to Cozy Corner. You're going to be wearing most of that."

"Ha, ha." Amelie swiped at her mouth with her napkin. "It's good, though. Want a bite?"

"I'll pass. I'm not in a big meat kind of mood."

"You're in some kind of mood. Something happen at work?"

Rachel put her fork down and steepled her hands over the takeout container. "I don't even know where to start."

"Why don't you start with the Yaris that's parked outside, a couple of slots down again?"

Rachel grimaced. "That's as good a place as any, I guess." While Amelie continued to eat, she relayed her conversation with Rainy, ending with, "I really felt like she was pushing me very hard into something I really didn't want."

"But, given that the Yaris is back, I'm taking it you took the job with them?"

"Sort of. Nothing is official yet. They've got to do some things to buy me out with Tech Temps, and there's some paperwork that needs filed, and so forth."

Amelie sat back in her chair; the messy burger temporarily forgotten. "So why did you agree to everything if you felt like you were being pushed into something?"

"Because it all made sense once I talked to Sherri."

"The one you like?"

Rachel nodded. "She explained that they use the phone gig to vet new couriers. And, before you say anything, I reminded her too that I'm an IT person, not a delivery person."

"And?"

"And she took me down to IT and introduced me around to the tech team. Their IT director said he'd seen my resume and he thought I'd be a good fit for them, but it would be about two months before he could bring me in there. They're restructuring the department right now. They know they're going to have some entry level slots to fill."

"What did you think of him? Of the other people there?"

"He seemed pretty straightforward. Older than I might have thought, but not old, you know what I mean? He's been with RHS for about seven years, almost since they started. There are maybe a dozen other people right now. Nice office space. It's quiet with high walled cubicles. Big server room." She picked up her fork.

"So, you said yes?"

"How could I not? They're bumping my pay up now... well, once Tech Temps is out of the picture. Plus, I have the Yaris to use until I move into IT, and we can use it for groceries and such. I get 100 miles a week in deviation from delivery routes."

"No more phones?"

"No. I'll be strictly a courier."

"But paid as if you're in IT? And they're applying for a visa for you? I don't think that's legal, Rachel." She dipped a fry in ketchup and jabbed it in the air. "I'm pretty sure you have to be doing the work the visa is for."

"By the time all the paperwork goes through, I very well might be." She attempted to take a bite of her salad, but Amelie wasn't finished.

"You've got about 40 days left on your temporary working papers, right?"

Rachel sighed. "Right."

"And there's two months or so until you can move into IT?"

"Yes. That's what they told me." She pushed the salad away.

"Don't you think you ought to just wait until you can move into a slot there?"

"The way Sherri explained it, I'm okay doing what I'm doing now, until the visa actually comes."

"Granted, she's the HR person, but it all sounds very fishy to me. Promise me you'll be careful? You'll get out of there if there are any signs that they're not playing by the rules? Any *other* signs, anyway."

"I promise. Our wedding is in a couple of weeks. I don't want to do anything that would justify risking *that* visa status!

A week later...
City Clerk's Office

"I feel bad about us having to get married here after what we had planned," Rachel told Amelie. "None of your family is here."

Amelie patted her soon to be wife's hand where it lay limp on the hardwood bench where they were seated. "The only person important to me is right here. We were never planning a big wedding anyway, and we need to get your status settled as soon as possible. Keep you legal."

"Rachel Bacar and Amelie Laurente," a clerk called out.

Amelie hopped up from the bench and tugged Rachel up. "Right here. It's pronounced like Emily."

"You're next. Ready?"

Rachel swallowed hard as Amelie tugged her forward, but she managed a nod.

Two weeks later...

Rachel rubbed her stomach as she exited the Yaris. *Shouldn't have had that second burrito for lunch.* She blew out a heavy breath and willed her stomach to stop lurching. *Just one more delivery and then I can get home and get out of these tight slacks.*

The surgery center in Jamaica anchored one end of an old mini mall. Someone kept it well compared to the rest of the mostly empty structure. Her deliveries there seemed to be pretty frequent, but its saving grace for her was the large parking lot.

She bypassed the information desk when she went in, already familiar with where she was going.

The medical assistant in the office she dropped off the square package no longer than the length of her hand smiled through her sliding window at her. "You again."

"Yes. This facility seems to be on my regular route."

"We had another driver for a while. An older, white-haired guy."

Rachel scrunched up her face. "Hmm. There aren't many of us. Four, that I know of and none of us have white hair."

"It's just as well. He seemed a little... cranky."

Rachel laughed, but then her stomach churned. She put a hand to it. "I really hate to ask this," she said. "Is there a restroom I can use?"

"Oh, sure." The young woman pointed. "Take a left out the door and there's one just down the hall a few doors on the right."

"Thanks so much."

Rachel exited the restroom a little disoriented after losing most of her lunch. She glanced first right, then left. The hallway to her left looked more familiar, but windows down the hall on the right caught her eye. She checked around again.

Seeing no one paying her any mind, she turned right and walked down the hall toward the set of three connected windows set on the wall about waist high. They reminded her of the viewing windows outside a baby nursery.

She was disappointed to see curtains on the inside blocking the view of most of the expanse, except for a sliver of a couple of inches between the second and third panes. She peeked inside.

She saw a surgical suite with a full complement of medical staff inside working around a person on an operating table. A man in scrubs was standing at one end of a table with trays of instruments. She was sure the box he had in front of him was the one she'd just delivered.

She watched in fascination as he opened it and took out a small foam container. He opened the container to reveal still more packaging.

Some kind of device? Why the foam? Protection?

Rachel shifted from foot to foot as she waited, hoping to glimpse what was in the packaging. She grew still as the man glanced her way, but he went right back to his task.

He half turned, held up the packaging, and appeared to say something to a man standing on the other side of the patient on the table. The second man nodded.

The first man turned back to the instrument table, laid some gauze down beside the foam container, choose an implement and slit the packaging open. A smokey haze billowed out of it. After waiting for the haze to clear, using an instrument, he took out what appeared to Rachel to be a human finger and laid it on the gauze.

Rachel shuddered. Her stomach churned as it had before.

She turned away from the window and rushed down the hallway to her left, past the bathrooms, and back outside.

She heaved for air, then threw up the rest of the contents of her stomach.

∼

"I delivered a finger!" Rachel said for a second time as she paced the floor in front of her wife.

Amelie, eyes wide, shook her head. "You're sure it was from the package you delivered?"

"Ninety-nine percent sure. It sure looked like it."

"Wow. Do you, uh... Do you think there have been body parts in any of the other packages you've delivered?"

Rachel smoothed over her braids. "Maybe. I don't know. Who knows?"

"Does everything go to medical offices?"

"No. Not even half from what I can gather, and a lot of what I deliver are just envelopes. A lot of offices downtown in high-rise buildings. Sometimes to a residence."

"Are the ones that go to offices near hospitals?"

Rachel shrugged. "Some. Maybe most. There are so many hospitals."

"X-rays, maybe?"

Rachel shrugged again. "I don't think so. Not everything is as big as those would be."

"On CD?"

"Who uses CDs anymore?"

"Good point," Amelie said.

Rachel sat down on the floor out in front of the sofa, cross-legged, cross armed, and rocked her body.

"Baby, you're getting yourself all worked up again."

"It was a finger, Amelie! They're trafficking body parts!"

Amelie got up and went behind Rachel. She put her hands on her wife's shoulders, stilling her. "I admit, I'm skeptical of some things they've done, but accusing them of trafficking might be jumping to conclusions."

"If it's not trafficking, why is it all so hush-hush? Why aren't the couriers told what they're delivering? I'm getting paid $30.00 an hour to keep me happy and going, is what I'm thinking. And why is everything in the RHS building so locked down? I have access to the floor I work out of, the lobby, and the garage. That's it. I can't even get back up to the floor I started on."

"Security?" Amelie guessed. "In a business like that, I'm sure there are a lot of issues, regulations—"

Her mind flashed back to the day the courier came onto the executive floor. *He had access.* "Or they're hiding something."

"Or that."

"You were against this from the start. Now it sounds like you're defending them."

Amelie let go and moved around in front of Rachel. She spoke in measured words. "Sort of. Not really. I was leery of them from the start, yes, but that was because they weren't telling you anything. The finger concerns me, but that could be legit. I'm still concerned about this whole H1B Visa business. You've got, what, a couple of weeks or so left on your temporary work permit?"

Rachel nodded.

"Any word from them about the status of the H1B?"

"Only what I've told you. They filed the paperwork."

"And a slot for you in IT?"

Rachel admitted she'd heard nothing.

Amelie grew quiet, eyes closed, thinking for several long seconds before expressing what she was thinking. "The more I think about it, the more I think you should quit."

"Do you think I should report them?"

"Report them to who? Based on what evidence?"

Rachel waggled her fingers at Amelie.

Amelie shook her head. "You'd need more than that to get anyone to take you seriously. But quitting is definitely an option." She held out a hand to Rachel. "Come on. Get up and go get on your computer. Start digging again, researching. There's got to be something out there about them. I'm sure there are licensing requirements and such for dealing in digits."

"That's not funny."

"I wasn't trying to be."

"Were you up, searching, all night?" Amelie asked.

"Most of it. I laid down for a couple of hours, but I couldn't sleep, and I didn't want to wake you, so I got back up."

"Find anything?"

"Not more than some normal business filings with the state and the city. There are so many databases I can't get into without password access or paying for access."

"A lot of the paid stuff is scam stuff."

"I'm sure," Rachel said. "I found one thing that was interesting, though. There was an article from about nine years ago about how Helena's husband was killed in a head-on collision and their toddler daughter survived, but she suffered serious injuries. She was in the back seat."

"And probably in a car seat."

"I assume. The article didn't give her age."

"A toddler would be two or three years old."

"It doesn't say what her injuries were, and I can't find anything else. The filings show the three women didn't start the business until more than a year after that accident. What if...

what if the injuries to Helena's daughter are what got her started in this business?"

"There might be something to that, but how would you ever find out short of asking Helena and giving away what you know?"

Rachel couldn't stifle a yawn.

"Call off, babe," Amelie begged, changing tactics. "You're tired. You don't need to be driving today. Or, just quit, like we talked about. Don't show up at all."

"I can't just quit."

"Why not? Look, I admire your work ethic, but we're doing okay and something in IT will come along soon now that we can get your work permit renewed."

Rachel pointed toward the living room window. "The Yaris. It's outside. I have to take that back there, if nothing else."

"Do you really feel up to driving?"

"I'll be fine."

"I'm so sorry. I'm married now and my... my wife and I are trying to plan long term." She realized she was rambling, and she tried to stop herself. "Anyway, I know you've spent some money pursuing a visa for me, and I appreciate that, but—"

Sherri's phone rang, interrupting her spiel. Sherri held up a finger as she took the call.

Rachel couldn't hear the other end of the conversation, but from Sherri's end, she could tell there was a delivery that needed made. Sherri was adamant. No one was available right away.

Why did I let Sherri talk me into another delivery? "This is taking forever," she said out loud to no one at all. "I should have quit like I intended to." *I just like her so much. I felt bad when she told me they didn't have anybody else.* "Last one. No more drives three blocks north, let alone all the way out here to Brentwood in the rain."

Her cell phone rang. *Amelie. Crap.* She punched accept and the speakerphone button. *Keep it legal.* "Hi hon."

"Hi yourself. Are you done? On the way home?"

"Um, not exactly. I agreed to take one last delivery. An envelope. No boxes."

"Rachel."

"They really didn't have anyone else."

Amelie sighed. When she finally spoke, she asked, "So, where are you now?"

Rachel glanced at the GPS display. "About ten minutes from my drop off in Brentwood, in decent weather, that is. It's pouring out here."

"Here too."

"It'll only take a minute once I get there, then it's back to the office to drop off the Yaris and home."

"So, like two-and-a-half hours?"

"Probably. Or even three with all the rain."

"Call or text me when you're leaving there and when you're leaving the office. I'm worried about you."

"I love you. It will be okay."

"I love you too, and I hope so."

Rachel estimated she'd been back on the expressway for fifteen minutes and had managed a couple of miles in the deluge when Amelie's answering text to hers came in. She tried to ignore it, knowing texting and driving were against the law, but she wanted to let Amelie know the weather was making things a lot slower going than she had imagined.

She picked up the phone and dialed Amelie, knowing she probably wouldn't be able to answer. *I'll just leave a quick message.*

"You're awake."

Rachel turned her head slowly toward the sound of Amelie's voice. She tried to speak, but she couldn't.

"Don't talk just yet. You've been in a sort of coma. The hospital put you in it on purpose for the past couple of days."

She tried to form the words 'hospital' and 'coma' with her lips, but her mouth was so dry she couldn't.

Amelie let go of her right hand and pushed a button somewhere near Rachel's head. She reported to the female voice that answered, "Rachel's awake."

The attending physician explained they'd had to amputate her left hand at the wrist. "There was too much damage to save it."

As Rachel tried to take that in, he went on. "There's somewhat better news on your left leg. You've got some rods and pins, but you should be able to make a full recovery with a lot of therapy."

Rachel tried to raise her left arm.

"Don't babe," Amelie said. "It's strapped down."

"Left-handed. How—"

"I know. Lots of therapy to learn to use your right and maybe a prosthetic for your left."

"Can't pay."

The doctor said, "Your father has taken care of everything."

Rachel looked at Amelie.

"I think your mother is behind it, but he's right."

"The police officer who was here to write a report said you went left of center and into the path of an oncoming car."

Rachel tried to shake her head. "No." She managed. "Expressway. It's divided. Not possible."

"There are photos of the mangled car, babe. I'm just happy you're still here with me."

Rachel shook her head again. "Raining so hard. I was crawling along on the right."

"Try not to talk."

She tried to sit up. "Car came out of nowhere. Off a ramp?"

Amelie shrugged.

"It hit me from the right," she insisted.

Amelie was just as firm. "There are pictures of the Yaris. All the damage is on the left; the driver's side."

"Not possible."

Rainy breezed into the room shortly after Amelie stepped out in search of a strong cup of coffee. "Pardon the intrusion. Your wife called about an hour ago and said you were awake."

Her voice was getting stronger with each small sip of water. "I'm so sorry about the car. I... I'll repay you, repay RHS."

Rainy waved her off. "We're far more concerned about you than about the car. How are you feeling?"

She tried to shrug, but the pain stopped her.

Rainy winced visibly. "That bad, huh?"

Rachel gave her a slight head nod instead.

"Do you feel up to signing some things? If you like, we can wait for your wife to come back, and she can help you read them."

"What things?"

"Well, we have insurance, of course, to cover the car and our employees and such. The insurance company needs a statement from you."

"My bills are paid."

Rainy held out a hand. "That may be the case, but you were

injured while you were working. There will be a workman's comp case filed. Your medical bills would be paid, and it would compensate you for your lost wages, unless you're found liable for the accident."

"Amelie says the police are saying I was at fault. I wasn't."

"There will be an investigation, of course. Unless..." She trailed off.

"Unless what."

"Unless you're willing to just settle with RHS for a lump sum."

"What?"

"We're prepared to accept... well, to pay you now, to keep this from being tied up for months as a workman's comp case. You'll have the money to take care of all of your needs during your rehabilitation. That's really better for you. And, when you're better, you still have a job with us... if you like."

Something doesn't sound right. "I... I don't know."

"$500,000. That's what I can offer you."

Rachel swallowed hard.

"Sounds to me like you don't want to be sued," Amelie said as she walked back into the room, a cup of coffee in hand.

Rainy turned toward her. "Not at all. I was simply explaining to Rachel how tedious the workman's compensation system is. I'm offering her the chance to bypass all of that."

Rachel raised the cup to her lips and took a small sip while both women watched her. She lowered it, transferred it to her right hand then went to Rachel's bedside and grasped her right hand with her left. She raised the hand. "She's going to have to go through some pretty serious rehab to learn how to use this hand to do things. She's... she was left-handed."

"As are you?" Rainy asked.

"Yes. That's how we met. We were both trying to take a seat

at the left end of a table at a group gathering while we were in school."

"Ah, and what do you do for work, Amelie?"

"I'm a graphic designer."

"So a creative type. You use your hands a lot."

"In a manner of speaking, yes. I do most of my work on a computer."

"Using both hands."

"Yes. Where are you going with this?"

"The fact is, I seem to be talking myself into talking with my business partners and offering Rachel more. Just as your hands are important to you, we know how important they are to a programmer." She paused and tapped her fingers against the document case she carried. "I think I can get them to agree to $750,000."

Rachel looked at Amelie. "Was that whole conversation weird to you?"

"Totally."

"I've got a terrible feeling that my accident was no accident."

"Me too."

"What do we do?" Rachel asked.

"I don't know. Call your father? See what strings he can pull with the police? Get what they know?"

"And I don't know about that. He's not a diplomat here anymore. Hasn't been for a few years. He doesn't have any pull with them."

"But maybe he knows someone who does."

"I'll think about it." She yawned.

"You're tired. You're overdoing it just coming awake and all."

"And you're overdoing it hanging out here. Go home. Get some rest. Go to work tomorrow, even. If we don't take their deal, we're going to need your paychecks."

Amelie yawned, too. "I hate to do it and leave you here all alone, but I know you're right." She leaned over and kissed Rachel gently. "Need anything from home? Looks like you're going to be stuck here a few more days."

Rachel held back a groan. "One or two of my silk headscarves." She fingered the hospital provided cap that looked like the toe of a pair of pantyhose. "This isn't working for me."

Amelie turned the wrong way, getting off the elevator. She realized her mistake when she passed the visitor waiting room she'd spent a couple of hours sleeping in while Rachel had been in her induced coma. *Long way around. Oh well.*

The sound of a man and a woman talking filtered out of a room a few more doors down. The woman's voice said, "Black or white, left hand dominate specimens command a premium."

He answered, "I won't do it. It's too risky."

"We paid you a cool million for Bacar. We could get you the same for the other."

Amelie backpedaled quietly for several steps, turned, and all but ran the other direction to Rachel's room. She opened the door, but stopped short just inside when she saw the Bacar's standing over her wife, on the other side of the bed, examining the wrapped stump at the end of her left arm.

Rachel's mother, Noura, noticed her and beckoned her into the room. She left her daughter's side, seeming to glide to the end of the bed in her traditional chiromani and shawl. "Amelie, good to see you." She held out a hand.

Still winded from her jog, she sucked in a breath and acknowledged her now in-laws. "Mr. and Mrs. Bacar." She moved toward Noura and grasped the offered hand. "I wish it was under better circumstances. I... I'm surprised to see you."

Salim Bacar clucked his tongue. "Of course we've come."

"Salim." Noura spoke only his name.

"Are you all right, Amelie?" Rachel asked.

Amelie made a quick decision. Addressing the Bacar's, she said, "We need to get her out of here, all of us out of here, fast. I mean like right now."

"But why?" Noura asked.

"No time to explain. Mr. Bacar, can you arrange it?"

Salim spread his hands. "We've only just arrived from the airport."

Noura gripped Amelie's hand tightly and shot her husband a look. "Salim will make it happen."

Before anyone could say anything else, there was a tap on the door. Without waiting for an invitation, the door swung open, and a well-dressed, heavy-set woman entered.

"Sherri!" The smile in Rachel's voice was obvious to Amelie.

"Hi there," the woman said.

Amelie recoiled at the voice and gave a worried look to Noura. *I know that voice.*

Rachel, forgetting the distress of moments before, introduced the other woman around as Sherri Trainor, the head of HR for RHS.

When the introductions were complete, Sherri said, "I'm so sorry to intrude. I'm here because... Well, let's just say I'm sorry for the confusion Rainy caused yesterday. We should never have sent a money manager out to do something that requires a more human touch." She smiled at her own attempt at humor.

"And what was that?" Salim asked.

"Salim, is it?"

"Ambassador Bacar," Noura supplied.

Amelie did her best to play along with the slight deception of Salim's current status.

Sherri looked momentarily taken aback. Recovering, she

stammered, "We, uh, we need Rachel's signature on some paperwork, ambassador, so we can begin the claims process on the Yaris she was driving, and—" She drew in a breath and smiled at Rachel. "And we were attempting to negotiate a settlement with your daughter."

Noura raised an eyebrow. "A settlement?"

Salim waved his wife off. "A monetary settlement? Without the advice of counsel?"

"She would have counsel in the workman's comp system—"

"Which you were trying to avoid," Amelie supplied.

"There will be no settlement," Salim proclaimed. "We'll retain counsel for her."

After Salim Bacar shot down any thoughts of a settlement with Rachel and shuffled the RHS owner out of his daughter's hospital room unceremoniously, Amelie and Rachel filled the Bacars in on events with RHS since Rachel's employment.

"There's more," Amelie admitted to a skeptical Salim. She told the other three what she'd overheard Sherri say, then pointed at Rachel. "That's why we need to get her out of here."

Noura asked, "You're sure?"

"About what I heard?"

"That it was this Sherri person?"

"Yes. Positive."

"This is all very far-fetched," Salim said.

Noura rose from the lone visitor chair she'd been sitting in. "I believe them. We must help them."

"Did you know my parents were coming?" Rachel asked Amelie when the Bacars stepped out in search of food.

Amelie shook her head. "I tried to call your mom last night, after I left here. Nothing. They must have been in the air."

"I don't want my father moving me from here."

"Babe, I don't think you're safe here."

"He'll take me to the embassy."

"You're too injured for that."

"It doesn't matter to him. And *you* can't go. By the sound of it, you aren't safe here either. It sounds like Sherri is... is... I don't even know."

"Sherri, Rainy, all of them."

Rachel's brown eyes grew enormous. She tried to shift around in the bed until Amelie laid a hand on her, stilling her. "I just remembered something! Something about Sherri!"

"Huh?"

"Sherri wasn't on any of the business filings, just the CEO Helena and the CFO Rainy. Sherri told me my first day her real name is Shirley. I researched her as Sherri Trainor, not Shirley Trainor."

Amelie pulled out her phone and started a Google search. Several minutes later, she handed her phone to Rachel.

"What did you find?"

"Just read it. Then, let's call Sherri and get her back in here, say tomorrow, to give us some time. Remind her you still haven't signed that insurance claim form and tell her your father doesn't make your decisions. You're going to take her deal. That should buy us some time. I have an idea that just may work."

Even after Rachel called Sherri, Amelie felt ill at ease leaving the room alone. She stuck to the high traffic brightly lit corridors other than the one her wife's room was on.

Noura and Salim Bacar came off the elevator as she stood in front of it and considered the possible safety factors involved in taking it downstairs as a woman, alone, knowing there was someone on the staff who felt justified in taking limbs for cash. She blew out a breath she hadn't realized she was holding and smiled. "Just the two I was looking for."

Salim's brow furrowed, but Noura smiled back at her and asked, "Is everything all right dear?"

"It will be. I think. Let's take a ride to another floor, and I'll explain."

"And leave my daughter alone?" Noura asked.

Salim stepped back in the elevator. "Let's get this over with; hear what she has to say."

In a quiet family waiting room off a surgical unit for heart patients, she whispered to the two of them what they'd learned since they left the room. Salim nodded along but didn't comment until she passed her phone to him, and he read what she and Rachel had for himself.

"It's compelling," he said, "but it's not enough, not for the American police or American courts."

"That's where we come in. All of us." She swallowed and began. "Who do you know on the NYPD, Mr. Bacar?"

He spread his hands. "I've been out of diplomatic service for several years now. That ruse will only take us so far."

"No ruse. Just someone who will take a quick look at something that we can trust to give us an honest answer."

Salim tapped a finger on his chin. "There are a couple of people. At least one is still with the police, I believe."

"Do you think he'd be willing to show up here tomorrow, too?"

Her father-in-law shrugged. "I've no idea."

"Ask him," Noura implored her husband.

"Fine. I'll do it. But if we don't get the answers we seek, we do not go through with any crazy plans."

Amelie nodded. "Of course not."

"What can I do?" Noura asked.

"Actually, there's one thing, if you feel up to it?"

"Anything."

"Walk with me past the office on Rachel's floor where I heard Sherri and a man talking. We need to figure out who she was talking to."

∼

Sherri breezed in, with Rainy following.

"Even better than we planned it," Amelie mouthed to Rachel.

Sherri frowned when she saw the Bacars were in the room. She shook visibly when a police lieutenant stepped out of the bathroom and blocked the only door out of the room.

"What's going on?" Rainy asked.

The lieutenant handed the two women some photos. "Do either of you recognize this car?"

Sherri closed her eyes, but Rainy studied the photos closely. "From the plate number, it appears to be the Yaris owned by RHS, our company." She waved a hand between herself and Sherri. "But all the damage is on the right side. I was told the damage was to the left side and the front end."

The lieutenant looked at Sherri. "I'm betting you can explain that, can't you Mrs. Trainor. Or should I call you Mrs. Hardin? Shirley Hardin?"

Sherri winced. "It's Trainor. I re-married a year ago… finally." She sighed and then whispered, "And now it's probably over."

"I'd say. Making a false police report. Insurance fraud. And, I hear that's just for starters."

Amelie stepped forward with printouts of the seven-year-old article about 'Shirley Hardin's Newest Venture' she'd found in her phone search the day before. "You lost your right hand twenty years ago in a horseback riding accident. You were married to Derek Hardin then, who was a biophysicist. He devoted years to studying the reattachment of limbs and re-animation after your accident, didn't he? At least, until he died under mysterious circumstances about eight years ago leaving you all of his life insurance."

"That's all true... at least about the biophysics and the re-animation," Sherri said. "I can vouch for that."

Rachel jumped in. "You two joined with Helena to form RHS, Reanimated Hand Specialists, didn't you?"

"Yes," Rainy said, speaking for both of them, her tone matter of fact. "We met Helena in a parent's support group. My son also lost his hand. His arm too. We each put in a stake to start the company. It took work, time, and a lot of patience as we built and proved our technology worked, but we've been very successful despite the skeptics, naysayers and--. Anyway, it's all legitimate and highly regulated. I'm not sure why we're here and why the law is involved." She looked at her co-owner when no one rushed to answer. "Care to enlighten me?"

Sherri pursed her lips and didn't say a word.

Rachel filled in the blanks. "It seems you may not have been successful enough for Shirley here. She got greedy. She started getting the hands and digits you needed to satisfy your clients in ways that weren't always from legitimate organ donors; ways that weren't always legal."

"I think I want a lawyer," Sherri said.

Rachel sighed. "You're going to need one."

∽

"Hey, you're back. It's been a few weeks," the medical assistant said to Rachel.

Rachel grinned. "In more ways than one." She turned on her crutches, took the package from Amelie, and handed it through the window. "That's precious cargo in there. It's my own. I'm your next patient, Rachel Bacar-Laurente."

ABOUT THE AUTHOR

Anne Hagan is the author of over twenty works of fiction in the mystery, romance, and thriller genres. She writes of family, friends, love, murder, and mayhem in no particular order and often all in the same story. She's a half owner of the weekly discount eBook newsletter, MyLesfic, a wife, parent, foster parent, and an Army veteran. She draws from all of those experiences when she writes because truth is often stranger than fiction.

1
CHECK ANNE OUT ON HER BLOG, ON FACEBOOK OR ON TWITTER:

For the latest information about upcoming releases, other projects, sample chapters and everything personal, check out Anne's **blog** at https://AnneHagan-Author.com/ or like Anne on **Facebook** at https://www.facebook.com/AuthorAnneHagan. You can also connect with Anne on **Twitter** @AuthorAnneHagan.

2
JOIN ANNE'S EMAIL LIST

Are you interested in **free books**? How about **free short stories**? For those and all the latest news on new releases, **opportunities to get review copies of all of her new releases** and more, please consider joining Anne's email list at: https://www.AnneHaganAuthor.com by filling in the pop up or using the brief form in the sidebar.

ALSO WRITTEN BY THE AUTHOR

The books of the Morelville Mysteries series Anne's WLW themed mystery/romance series:

RELIC: **The Morelville Mysteries–Book 1**–The first Dana and Sheriff Mel mystery and the first book in the Morelville saga. Please click the link above, which will take you to Anne's site, where you can get links to get this book.

CASES COLLIDE **for two star crossed ladies of law enforcement!**

BUSY BEES: **The Morelville Mysteries–Book 2**

ROMANCE AND MURDER **Mix in the Latest Story Featuring Sheriff Mel Crane and Special Agent Dana Rossi!**

DANA'S DILEMMA: The Morelville Mysteries–Book 3–The relationship matures between Mel and Dana in an installment that features a breaking Amish character, an ex-girlfriend, a conniving politician, and murder.

ELECTIONS AND OLD Loves Combine with Deadly Results in a Romantic Mystery Featuring Sheriff Mel Crane and Special Agent Dana Rossi!

HITCHED AND TIED: The Morelville Mysteries–Book 4

MEL AND DANA attempt to bring their growing romantic relationship full circle, but family, duty, and family duties all conspire to get in the way.

A DELAYED HONEYMOON getaway takes a deadly turn for newlyweds Mel and Dana; meanwhile, two meddling mothers won't let sleeping fisherman lie in the latest Morelville Mystery.

A Crane Christmas: The Morelville Mysteries–Book 6

Is it the Christmas season or the 'silly season'?

Mad for Mel: The Morelville Mysteries–Book 7

Rival gangs will stop at nothing to gain sole control of the drug trade in Muskingum County, and they've picked Valentine's week to create a firestorm of murder and mayhem as they battle each other for supremacy.

HANNAH'S HOPE: The Morelville Mysteries–Book 8

A YOUNG MOTHER with a troubled past seeks help from Mel and Dana, but is their effort to assist her too little, too late?

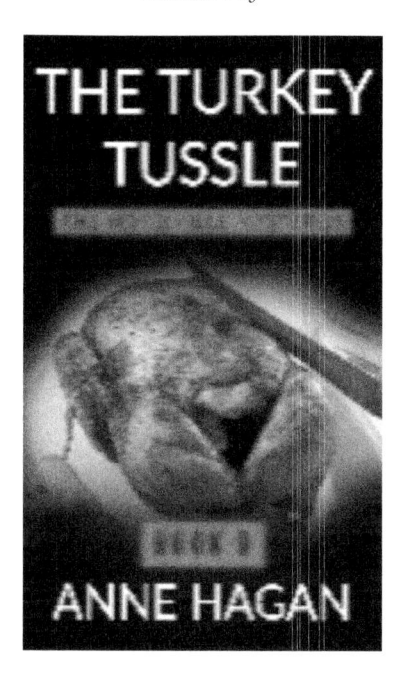

THE TURKEY TUSSLE: The Morelville Mysteries–Book 9

THE OLD-FASHIONED COUNTRY village of Morelville holds a secret.

SULLIED SALLY: The Morelville Mysteries–Book 10

AN UNSOLVED MURDER, over 40 years in the past, leads to the discovery of a new victim and the return of an old stalker.

Finding Sheila: The Morelville Mysteries–Book II

A WOMAN, imprisoned for manslaughter, disappears without a trace during transport between states, and it's all up to Dana to find her.

TENNESSEE BOUND: The Morelville Mysteries–Book 12

THE POLITICS and the paper-pushing are wearing on Sheriff Mel. Will she chuck it all?

∽

A SPINOFF from the Morelville Mysteries series, The Morelville Cozies series feature meddling mother sleuths Faye Crane and Chloe Rossi getting mixed up in mysteries all their own.

THE PASSED PROP: The Morelville Cozies–Book 1

CHLOE ROSSI WANTS to retire with her husband and move away from suburban sprawl to bucolic Morelville; the only trouble is, Morelville is experiencing its worst crime wave ever, and Marco Rossi wants no part of a move there. What to do?

Opera House Ops: The Morelville Cozies–Book 2

Murder and other sinister goings-on at a vacant 1800s era opera house in Morelville and a modern-day property developer who wants to raze the historic building for his own gain have the village residents all tied up in knots and Faye Crane trying to play savior to history.

∽

Three multi-eBook boxed sets of the Morelville Mysteries works by Anne Hagan are also available for purchase.

THE
MORELVILLE
MYSTERIES
ANNE HAGAN
RELIC
BUSY BEES
DANA'S DILEMMA
HITCHED AND TIED

THE
MORELVILLE
MYSTERIES
ANNE HAGAN

THE MORELVILLE MYSTERIES **Full Circle Collection** is a five eBook set that contains the first four Morelville Mysteries novels and an exclusive Companion Guide that is only available with this set.

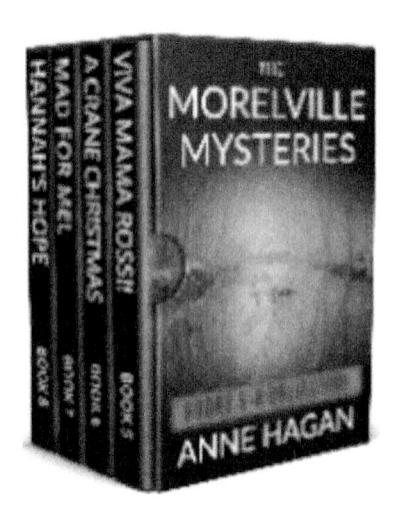

THE MORELVILLE MYSTERIES: Books 5-8 Collection

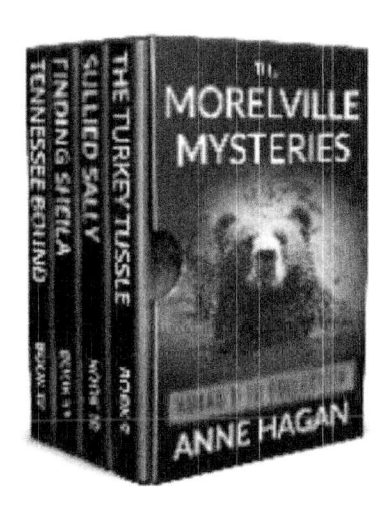

THE MORELVILLE MYSTERIES: Books 9-12 Collection

STEEL CITY CONFIDENTIAL–ANNE'S first legal thriller

CLIENTS HIDE things from their lawyers all the time. Pam Wilson makes it an art form.

∽

ANNE ALSO WRITES ROMANCE!

Broken Women

CAN TWO WOMEN, **unlucky in love, find solace in each other?**

WHERE DO you go when you lose everything? Who do you turn to next when nobody seems to want you for more than a casual fling?

HEALING EMBRACE–THE stand-alone sequel to Broken Women

BARB AND JANET WERE A COUPLE... and then they weren't. What now?

STEAMBOAT REUNION–THE third and final book in the Barb and Janet series

CAN YOU GO HOME AGAIN?

Loving Blue in Red States

A LESFIC ROMANCE *short story* series that kicks off with a visit to the little town of Sweetwater, Texas. It's followed by stops in Birmingham, Alabama, Jackson Hole, Wyoming, Perryville, Missouri, Salt Lake City, Utah, Savannah, Georgia, Wall, South Dakota and East Tennessee. More stories will follow for as long as there are 'Red States' in the United States. There's also an international contribution to the series, Kilbirnie Scotland authored by Kitty McIntosh.

A Sweetwater Christmas

Traditional and progressive meet in ruby red west-central Texas...

This novella is a significant expansion of the short story, Loving Blue in Red States: Sweetwater Texas.

Christmas Cakes and Kisses

Two different worlds **brought together by cake...**

This is a sweet romance featuring a character from Anne's popular Morelville Mysteries series. The book stands alone.